Christmas Capers

VIKKI WALTON

Copyright @2020 by Vikki Walton

Morewellson, LTD.
P.O. Box 49726
Colorado Springs, Colorado 80949-9726

ISBN: 978-1-950452-10-1 (standard)

ISBN: 978-1-950452-14-9 (large print)

Front Cover: DLR Designs

Editing: Underwraps Publishing

Formatting: Wild Seas Formatting

Christmas Capers

A

Backyard Farming

Mystery

BOOK 4

VIKKI WALTON

Morewellson, Ltd.

Chapter One

Anne plopped down on the chair and flung her arms out to her sides, "Ugh ... so tired."

Kandi looked up from the box of Christmas decorations she was going through. "Tired? From what? Oh wait, is that due to your, like, hormonally-thing?"

Anne threw a red and green plaid Christmas pillow at Kandi. "No, it's not like my 'hormonally-thing.'" She made air-quotes with her fingers. Though she did need to go see Hope about more herbal tea. She had been tossing and turning at night and noticed some more night-sweats.

"Good, because this is the most fantabulous time of the year." Kandi unwrapped another piece of Anne's Christmas village, cooing over the piece as she set it on the table next to other pieces. Anne rubbed her hands along the sides of the green overstuffed chair and pondered how Kandi had kept her childhood enthusiasm for Christmas. The young woman exuded energy and happiness while Anne herself actually felt no Christmas spirit.

She raised herself up, "We just finished decorating the bed and breakfast. I don't see why I have to decorate my space. It's just me … oh, and Spencer." She needed to make an effort for him. Although he'd already decorated his room so shouldn't that give her a pass? She sighed and fell back in the chair before glancing out the window. The skies for the last few days had been overcast and gray. With Colorado having sunny days practically year round, Anne wondered if that's what had her in the doldrums. "Looks like we may get snow soon."

"We may actually get snow for Christmas." An excited squeaky noise escaped Kandi's lips as she bounced up and down in joy. She pulled a snowman from the box and began carefully unwrapping it from the bubble wrap. "I still think that maybe your peri-pause is acting up again."

"It's peri-menopause and it's not 'acting up' either. Hope has seen to that. She's really a whiz with her herbal tinctures and teas."

"Well, I know it's something. Hmm ..." Kandi wiggled her eyebrows. "You're missing your boyfriend."

"He's not my ... geez, you make it sound like we're kids or something." Anne rose and moved toward the table. Carson had taken some time off and his absence was definitely noticed by her.

Kandi cocked her head to one side; a habit Anne had seen on many occasions since meeting the young woman. She had first been Anne's quirky neighbor and was now so much more than that. To think that a chain of horrible events had led them to come together.

Anne smiled and hugged Kandi. "You know I love you. You're a bit of fresh air for my doldrums."

"Ah, I love you too. But no

getting out of this!" She shook her finger at Anne.

Anne looked at the boxes of stuff still to be unpacked, "How about we do this later? I know you're busy with the town decorating committee."

"Oh no you don't! You're not, like, getting off that easy. We're doing this." She pulled a garland out that tinkled with Christmas bells and shone with fake candy ornaments.

A black shape flew up on to the table toward them, batting at the closest shiny item. "No Mouser!" Anne was quick to scoop the cat up before he was able to pull the ornaments off the garland. She stroked his fur, but he fought to return to his new toy. "See, there's no way that he's going to leave the decorations alone, much less a Christmas tree."

"We'll figure something out. Now back to the boyfriend. When is Sheriff Carson coming back to town?"

"Soon I hope. He said that since he's visiting back home, he's had lots of invites from family that haven't seen him in ages, plus old friends."

"Like old girlfriends?"

"Well, he said he was meeting a group of college buddies and yes, an old girlfriend is in the mix." Anne pulled a string of lights from another box and plopped down in a chair to work on making sure none were broken.

Kandi searched Anne's face before saying, "Ah, you don't have anything to worry about."

"I'm not worried." Anne looked up at Kandi which wasn't difficult as she was short and petite. Anne smiled as the picture of a little gnome went through her mind. "Okay, maybe a little."

She set the lights to the side. Mouser immediately hopped up and planted his bottom on top of them. "Mouser, go away."

He proceeded to groom his paw. "I see who's the boss here!" Kandi laughed as she lifted him up and took him back to the kitchen.

"It's your fault. You're the one

who gave that rascal to me."

"I bet, like, you're glad now though, aren't you?" Kandi returned and hoisted another box onto the dining room table.

"Yes, you got me there. He's earned his keep. No mice." She rapped on the wood table with her knuckles. The Victorian house she'd purchased on moving to Carolan Springs had been a great project for her, and it was almost finished. The third floor was the last portion of the remodel. Since it had been vacant, Mouser had done an excellent job on putting out the 'no vacancy' sign for any mouse that dared to enter and try to build a new condo.

"I think you're just bored. You need a project to keep you busy. I guess you, like, can't help being a workaholic."

"I'm not a workaholic and you're starting to use 'like' in every sentence again. You know how that 'like' drives me crazy."

Kandi winked. "Maybe I'm doing it on purpose."

"Oh you." She hit Kandi's arm with an elf hat with big green ears.

"I love that. Give it here!" Kandi took it over to a nearby mirror and tried it on. "What do you think?" She struck a pose.

"Of course, you would. It looks like it was made for you. But why shouldn't it? You're an elf disguised as a human."

"Hmmm, we need help coming up with our theme this year for the town. You need to join us!"

"No." Anne shook her head. "I

have no desire whatsoever to be on a committee." She made a point of acting like a shiver had gone down her spine.

"Come on. It'll be fun! Eliza's doing it."

"Really?" Anne wondered why Eliza de French, a beautiful Ethiopian hand model, would volunteer to sit on the town's Christmas décor committee. "I didn't realize she was back from her modeling assignment in Madrid." She crossed her arms. "Who else is on the committee?"

Kandi checked off names on her fingers, "Eliza, Polly, Molly, Spencer ..."

"Spencer's doing it? He didn't say anything to me about it."

"I think it's so he can be close to Molly. I think he may have a crush on her." She tucked a lock of bright red hair behind her ear.

"That it?"

"A new person. Um, what's her name?" She tapped her chin with her finger. "I can't remember, but she works at the jewelry shop in town. They're going to be providing the tree for the lighting." She stopped for a moment before continuing, Oh, and Stanley. I wanted to get a good combination of old and young folk for their input. So, you'd fit in, right in the middle." She smiled and Anne shook her head at her.

"So, age is how you're setting up the committee? Don't you think—"

"I'm missing someone." Kandi interrupted and counted on her fingers again. She tapped her finger on her chin. "Let's see ..." and she went through the names again. "I know there's someone else as we have seven on the committee so far."

Anne sighed, "Did you count yourself?"

Kandi giggled, "Oh, yeah, me!" She yelled back over her shoulder as she moved into Anne's kitchen, heading for the fridge. "So, you'd make eight." She swiveled as if her current thought process had left. "I want hot chocolate. How about you?"

"Sure." Anne followed Kandi into the kitchen where she sat in one of the wooden kitchen chairs. She felt feet hop onto her lap. "Hello, Mouser." He kneaded biscuits with his paws on her pants before he twirled around a few times, settling into a ball on Anne's lap. As she stroked the cat, a loud purr emanated through the room. "How about I think it over?"

"I think it would be good as it would give us an eighth person and help divide the work more evenly."

Anne watched as Kandi stirred the milk in a pan on the stove. Glancing out the window, she spied soft snowflakes falling outside. Two figures passed in front of the door, and she felt the cold as they hurried in from outside. Spencer bolted into the room while Stewart closed the door behind him, sealing them in the warmth of the kitchen.

Spencer removed his red beanie, now wet from the snow, and shook his dark locks out. He shoved his hand through his hair before opening the fridge to grab a meat and cheese tray. "Gotta run. Our game's starting soon." He gave Anne a peck on the cheek before scooting up the stairs.

Anne laughed at how attached she'd grown to the young man who'd escaped the horrible foster group home he'd been in before moving in with her. Never in a million years would she have guessed she'd have a teenager in her home. When Carson was here it almost felt—

"Anne?" Stewart had hung his

coat on the hook and was speaking to her.

"Oh, sorry. I didn't hear you. What did you say?" She accepted the cup of steaming hot chocolate topped with fresh whipped cream and sprinkles. Kandi set another cup in front of Stewart who kissed Kandi on the top of her head. "Thanks, hun. Hits the spot."

Anne took a sip of the hot chocolate and marveled at how Kandi could always get it just right. Not too sweet, but not bitter either. "Kandi, this is delicious. I agree, it's perfect for right now." She cupped the mug.

"Remember Deputy Ruiz?" Stewart unwrapped the plaid scarf from around his neck and placed it next to his jacket. "He told me that he thinks something is going on in town. Something criminal."

Anne's movement woke Mouser who jumped onto the table. Before she could grab it, the mug fell over, and hot chocolate spread across the table. "Oh, Mouser, no. Not my hot chocolate."

Kandi grabbed paper towels and the trio mopped up the spill before Kandi wiped it down with a wet cloth. "I'll make another one. No harm. No foul." She pulled milk from the fridge, but before moving to the stove spoke to Stewart, "Really? You know I heard a rumor that..."

"Now Kandi, you know I hate gossip."

"Yes, I know. If someone talks to you about others, you can be sure they talk about you. But I'm talking with you too, so it doesn't really matter." She grinned.

Anne sighed.

"You know you want to know as much as I do. You're, like, dying to solve another mystery!"

"I am not."

"You are too!" Kandi stuck her tongue out.

Stewart held up his hands in protest." Ladies! Can I continue?"

"Yes, but only when I get more hot chocolate."

Kandi set her cup in front of Anne. "Here, take mine. I want to know." She poured more milk in a pan and stirred it while waiting for Stewart to speak.

"From what I overheard ..." he took a sip of the hot chocolate before continuing, "Someone is stealing jewelry in town."

Anne pulled a face. "He told you that? That doesn't sound like Ruiz."

"No," he hesitated for a moment and glanced at Kandi. Anne turned to Kandi, but she'd already turned back to the stove. "I was doing some work at the bookstore, hanging lights. He walked by and was talking on his phone."

"That seems kind of weird."

Kandi interrupted. "Well, that's the way things are sometimes. You find out things in the weirdest ways." She sipped at her hot chocolate and Stewart also took a sip of his.

"I don't know. Are you all not telling me something? I feel like you're hiding something from me."

"What makes you say that!" They burst out in unison.

"That. For starters. You're both acting all weird. If I didn't know any better ..."

Stewart didn't reply but took a drink of his chocolate.

"There you go with that peri-pause stuff all over again. I think it's affecting your mind."

Stewart suppressed a chuckle and focused his attention on his hot chocolate.

"So, help me, if you say even

one word Stewart, I will bean you over the head with a plastic snowman."

He held up his hands in surrender before making a zipper motion in front of his mouth.

Anne's mind raced. Was there an actual jewel robber in their midst? It made no sense, but in another way it did. Tourists flocked to the small town for its annual Homesteading Festival and during the holiday season. While many would head to Colorado's big ski resorts, Carolan

Springs had kept its old world charm with an ice skating rink and a great tubing hill for kids. Sleigh rides were a crowd favorite as well as snowshoeing along the trail that leads to the lake. Even some of them dared a winter lake plunge. Best of all, they'd kept their prices manageable so that accommodations were often booked way in advance. Families who preferred a more laid-back atmosphere had made the town a wonderful winter holiday destination and the local Chamber had seen it as the opportunity to add to the town coffers.

Thus, with all the tourists, it made sense that a robber would go after small items that would be easy to steal and sell for a quick profit. While people were out and about, it would be fairly easy to get in and out of rooms carrying away small items like jewelry.

"Have you spoken to Carson about this?" Anne paced the room. "We need to make sure that our guests at the Brandywine Inn secure any valuables in the safe."

Kandi's head bobbed up and down. "Yes, that's important."

"You said Polly knew someone who'd had their jewelry stolen?"

"Yes. But I thought—"

"I'll go over and talk with her tomorrow."

"Or you can go with me to the committee meeting this evening. She'll be there and you can speak to her then."

"Good idea." Anne placed a finger over her lips and thought of the questions she needed to ask

Polly. "Also, didn't you say there was someone new, too? I'd like to meet them."

"You'll be on the committee then?" Kandi clapped her hands together.

"Well, I, uh ..." Anne sighed. "Fine, I'll be on the committee."

Stewart rose and emptied the last dregs of his hot chocolate. He rinsed the cup out and set it in the sink. "I need to get going. Lots of people wanting their lights put up before it gets crazy cold, so I have a busy day ahead of me." He put on his coat.

Kandi went over and hugged him before twisting the scarf around his neck. "Stay warm." Stewart kissed her and said, "See you later."

She smiled up at him before winking, "Thank you."

"My pleasure. Anything for you." He pulled a cap from his jacket pocket and put it on before heading back outside.

Kandi shut the door and waved after him as he moved out of view.

Anne rose and took her cup to the sink. "That man adores you. You need to marry him."

"Oh, I will. But men love the chase. You have to let them win you after all."

Anne laughed. "Really? How old are you compared to me? I'm double your age."

"Then you should know by now that you have to keep them on their toes." Kandi cocked her head again. "In fact, what would you think about dying your hair red for Christmas?"

"Are you crazy? No, I'm not dying my hair red."

"Sorcha's hair is a ..."

Anne bristled. "Oh, no you don't. Sorcha is a gorgeous Irish Sophia Loren and—"

"Do I detect a bit of jealousy?"

"Absolutely not."

"Um, okay ... Sure sounded like it. Must be that peri-pause thing again."

Anne threw the dishtowel at Kandi.

"So, are you happy?"

"What do you mean?" Anne picked up the towel from the floor.

"You have another case to solve."

"Well, I ... okay, yes, that makes me happy."

"Great. I gotta head home for a bit, but I'll pick you up at seven thirty for the committee meeting. Polly's hosting tonight over at her house behind the pet shop. We can talk over our plan while driving to the meeting."

"Fine. I'll walk over to your

house, and we can go from there." Anne hugged Kandi. "Thanks for caring for me so much. I'll try to work on the peri-pause. Maybe you're on to something there."

"Maybe."

Chapter Two

Anne and Kandi arrived just as the others were pulling up in front of the small house that stood behind main street. Homes here were much smaller in comparison to either Anne's or Kandi's large Victorians. While theirs had been the homes of the mine's owners, these homes had been owned by the merchants that supplied the needs of the small but growing town in the Colorado mountains during the gold rush.

Polly's house was a cute little three rooms up, three down affair, with the upper level's outside portion decorated with a scalloped board facade. The front porch had once boasted a low wall with flowers cut out of the wood. Except when Polly moved in, she'd replaced the old, worn boards with paw prints. It was easy to know exactly which house was

Polly's. She had décor up for Halloween that she kept up until Thanksgiving. These decorations included two big eyes where her upper windows were located along with bent black pipe to mimic whiskers. The kids of the town always loved Polly's house. If the kids brought their pets dressed up to her house on Halloween, then the pets also received treats. And being a smart businesswoman, Polly would also include a discount for Christmas purchases at the pet store along with a flyer about animals needing homes.

Anne noticed large boxes resting on the porch which she knew contained a big red bow and a fun Santa hat-looking decoration that would soon adorn the top of the house. She heard a car pull up behind them. It was Eliza's new Range Rover. The elegant woman exited the vehicle before making her way over to Anne and Kandi.

"Eliza. It's so good to see you. You've been gone way too long this time." Anne and the woman kissed each other on each cheek, a custom that Eliza had affected after her many global travels. As usual, the woman was dressed impeccably in an emerald cape with fur-capped collar and sleeves. Her gloves went up to her elbows and were burgundy with gold trim. Anne knew that on the insides they were lined with soft, warm cashmere.

"Anne, so very nice to see you once again. And Kandi too." Kandi giggled through the air-kissing.

"So how did you get roped into

this committee?" Anne laced her arm with Eliza's as Kandi raced on ahead to greet Polly who stood at her door, beckoning them inside. "Who else?" She motioned to Kandi. "She may be little, but she's a powerhouse when it comes to persuasion."

"You can say that again. She wouldn't take no for an answer. So, I figured it would be best if I just gave in. I'm hoping this will stop her from focusing on more work for me elsewhere."

Eliza laughed, showing her full

set of bright-white perfect teeth. "You are funny, my friend."

"Hey, you two, come on in!" Polly waved from the porch.

Inside Polly took coats and purses, hanging them on a large oak wall tree. She'd put a gate across the staircase. Only that didn't stop four dog heads from popping through the rails, tails wagging strongly, as they accepted head pats from everyone entering the room.

In the corner, Stanley crouched close to the fireplace, nudging the crackling wood with a poker. Kandi was speaking to a woman Anne didn't recognize. She spied Spencer and Molly over by themselves, heads down in that awkward teenage silence Anne recalled from her youth.

Kandi cleared her throat and faced the group. "Everyone, this is Margaret. She works at Jay's Jewelry on third. She's sitting in as they will be supplying the large tree for the town center and want to hear our ideas on decorations so that they can coordinate with us." She held up the palm of her hand and Margaret stepped forward.

Anne gauged her to be in her late twenties or early thirties. Her hair was cut in a chic bob with what looked to be the professional work of a stylist's highlights. "Hello everyone. My name is Margaret, but feel free to call me Maggie. I'm looking forward to working alongside you to create a festive look for the Springs holidays." She smiled and took a step back, but not before Anne noticed a beautiful gold bracelet inset with three diamonds and a large ruby ring on her right hand. It was beautiful and probably had a beautiful price to go with it too.

"Polly, thanks again for letting us meet here." Kandi clapped and everyone followed with polite approval.

Polly distracted the group from embarrassing her any further by waving toward the dining area adjacent to the living room. "Please, help yourself to snacks and drinks before we start."

Anne sidled up to Stanley who was still intent on fixing the fire. Finally satisfied, he struggled up from the floor. She knew better than to try helping him up as it would only serve to wound his ego. When he'd made it to a standing position, she smiled at the elderly gentlemen, "How have you been Stanley?"

"If I were any better, I'd be twins."

"Good to know." Anne nodded toward the table in the next room. "Care to escort a lady to the treats?"

He cocked his arm. "It would be my pleasure."

In the dining room, a buzz of chatter surrounded the table as people selected from an assortment of finger sandwiches, various dips, and bite-sized sweets of fudge, divinity, and caramel apple bites. Once everyone had settled, Kandi began the meeting.

"As you all know, we want to create a wonderful theme for our Christmas holiday cityscape. Unfortunately, we're behind the curveball on time since the original chair got a job offer in Texas.”

“Bah, too cotton-picking hot in Texas. Why would anyone want to live there?” Stanley crossed his arms. “This here’s God’s country.”

“Um, technically, if God made everything, then that includes Texas.” Spencer replied.

Anne’s eyes grew wide, and Spencer got the hint to say no more. The last thing they needed was to get Stanley upset, but the gentleman simply replied, “Just so, son. Just so.”

Kandi had moved to the corner step so everyone could see her. “Even though we’re behind we still have a few weeks to Thanksgiving. I know that’s not a lot of time. But you’re each so creative and inventive, let’s put our heads together to plan something fun. We don’t have to worry about major decorations and lighting as that stays the same every year to keep town costs down.”

She turned to Spencer. “Spence, could you pass these out

to everyone, please?"

He took the papers from Kandi's hand and passed them around the room. "What you'll see are the last three years of decoration and themes. As you can see, they're all fairly similar. A mish-mash of all kinds of things. I'd like ours to be more unique. Any thoughts?"

"What's wrong with doing it the same way? In my day, we didn't …"

"Thanks Stanley, that's why we want your input. What are the important things that we need to continue with this year?"

Anne had to hand it to Kandi. She'd done well by appeasing Stanley without causing any affront.

Stanley beamed. "You're welcome." He sat back, satisfied. "Proceed."

Anne turned to Maggie. "Do you have any idea for decorating the tree? That might help with some of our ideas."

Maggie twiddled with the ruby

ring on her finger. "From what I've heard thus far from Jay and others in the shop, the main things are that we'll have a pretty large tree. There will be large colored balls for the ornaments along with large gold and silver chain links for the garland. At the bottom, we thought of various sized boxes wrapped as presents. But other than that, we didn't want to get too far into it in case we needed to make changes for a particular theme."

"Thoughts anyone?" Kandi

looked to the group.

Eliza had removed her gloves and set down her cup on a nearby coaster. "When we celebrated Leddet ... I mean Christmas, when I was growing up, the most important part were the people being with you that you loved. Presents are fun—"

"... but presence is the most important." Anne interrupted. "Sorry, bad habit."

Eliza took Anne's hand. "Yes, the people in our lives who care for us are the best presents of all."

Tears pooled in her eyes.

Molly bobbed up and down in her seat, with her hand raised. "Oh, oh, I have an idea!"

"Just spit it out," Polly chuckled.

"We could decorate the town as presents. Each of the shops could have bows on them and we could put wrapped boxes on the sidewalk."

"I like that idea, Molly. Thanks for sharing." Kandi turned to the group, "Anyone else?"

Spencer cleared his throat. "Just thinking what you all said about presents and presence."

The room grew quiet as they waited on him to continue. Anne leant forward in her chair, as ideas begin to materialize in her mind.

He looked around the room, "Um, never mind."

"Let's hear it." Polly gestured. "I, for one, would like to hear your idea."

"Well, you know every year when we have the tree lighting?"

Everyone nodded in agreement.

"If we're going with a presence or presents theme, everyone in the town could receive a clear glass ornament. Then that night before we light the tree, they could bring the ornament with a picture of their family inside the ornament and hang it on the tree."

Kandi clapped her hands together. "I love that idea! It would get the whole town involved. We could have a theme around the people, um, like …"

"Your presence is our present." Anne quipped. "We could provide them at the inn, and I bet others would join in giving them to their guests too."

Spencer looked up from his phone. "How many would we need? I already did some preliminary research and found a bulk source that can ship this week."

"Awesome!" Kandi clapped her hands. "Spence, could you and Polly work on that since she holds the purse-strings?" They nodded in agreement.

"I love that idea. It's also a good tagline. We could even use that in marketing materials for the town." Polly sat on the Chamber board so Anne could see the wheels already turning.

"Here's another idea about the boxes on the street." Stanley spoke up.

"Yes?" The group replied in unison.

"Some could have mirrors inside them with tiny lights so the person standing inside looks like they're in a snow globe. Others could be where people could be framed for taking those selfish pictures." He folded his arms, satisfied with his inclusion in the planning.

Thankfully, no one dared to correct Stanley on the selfie pics, but chimed in that his ideas were good ones.

"We can certainly leave room all around the bottom of the tree for people to add in their ornaments to the tree. What would be your idea of allowing businesses to put ornaments on the tree with their logos?" Maggie chimed in.

"I don't know." Polly shook her head. "Commercialism seems to spoil so much."

"What if each business had to pay to be on the tree, it could only be their logo, and the money went to helping families in need over the holidays?" Spencer added. Molly took his hand, and his face went red.

Anne thought, Ah, young love.

It may be puppy love, but it's sure real to that puppy.

"That's a great suggestion. I could talk to Jay, and he could speak to other business owners about it. What do you think about that idea, Polly?" Maggie touched the ring on her finger.

"I could probably get behind that. I know the Chamber likes to do something similar. Let me talk to them and get some feedback on it first. Then I'll get back to you." She wrote on a notepad she held in her lap.

Stanley pushed himself up from the chair. "I've got to be getting home. I think that's enough for one evening." The others agreed and decided to meet back in a week after everyone had time to think through their discussion.

As they were wrapping up in their coats, Anne spoke to Maggie. "I love your bracelet. It's simple and elegant."

"You want it?" After noticing the confused look on Anne's face, she continued. "One of the best ways to show off our merchandise is to wear it, so others can see it."

"That's a good idea." She lowered her head and whispered to Maggie. "Have you heard about any jewelry robberies?"

"Robberies? No! When has this been happening?"

Kandi caught up to them. "Yes, we overhead something about them earlier. Maybe Jay knows more about it."

"I don't—"

Kandi responded, "Sorry, we're in a hurry. But I'll be happy to chat about it later. Bye!" She whisked Anne out the door.

"What was that all about?"

"Nothing. I just need to get home, that's all."

"Ah, is Stewart coming over this evening?"

Kandi shrugged her shoulders.

"All right. I don't want to be the one to thwart young love." She turned to wave goodbye to Eliza and Maggie who stood talking on the porch. They waved back before continuing their conversation. It was a bit strange that someone who worked for a jewelry store hadn't been informed about the robberies. Yet again, it could be, because it hadn't affected them. She might stop by the store tomorrow as she wanted to take another look at that bracelet.

Chapter Three

A few days later Anne found herself in Hope's Herbal Shoppe ordering tea and gathering more supplements. She and Hope had connected when she'd first moved to Carolan Springs and had become friends in the time since. Hope waved from behind the counter as she helped a woman trying to make up her mind between the various hand-milled soaps on display. Anne wandered the shop until the woman left, her hands now full of soaps and various other items she planned to gift to inn guests.

"Hey there, I see you have your hands full. Let me help." She took some items from Anne and placed them on the counter. Noticing the herbal tea, she held it up. "Are you having some issues again?"

"Uh, yeah. Some sweats at night and not sleeping too well."

"Do you need to come in for another check-up?" Hope queried.

"No, doc. I'm fine." Anne was

thankful that Hope was not only a certified herbalist but held a medical doctorate as well.

"Okay. But if it keeps up, set an appointment. Night sweats are no fun and not getting proper sleep can really affect your moods."

"Oh, no. Has Kandi been squealing on me?"

"No. But if she did, I'm sure that she has your best interests at heart." She rang up the items. "I'm about to take a break. Got time for a chat?"

"Sure." Anne waited until a young woman took over the counter in front before she followed Hope back through her office and into her personal living quarters. The television that used to sit front and center was gone as were many of the other items that used to be in the room. "How's Faith?"

"Mom is doing as well as expected. I've put as many familiar items as possible in her new room, so she feels secure." She set about making a fragrant tea as cinnamon filled the air.

"Hmm, that smells nice. What is it?"

"Some green tea, cinnamon, goji berries, and lemon. Do you want a drizzle of honey?"

"Yes, please."

Once they'd settled with their tea in two large comfy chairs, Anne turned to the question she'd been waiting to ask.

"Have you heard of any jewelry robberies in town?"

In response, Hope threw back

her head and laughed heartily. "Oh my gosh. I should have seen your flushed cheeks and knew what that meant. You're excited that there may be another mystery to solve."

"Well, I ... okay, you got me. I've been bored. The house is pretty much done. I've closed up any more remodeling until next year. I'm starting to plan the garden, but I can only do so much with that. Now that we've hired on more help at the B&B, I'm twiddling my thumbs."

"What about writing another book?" Hope sipped at her tea.

"I don't know. I'm not feeling the desire to do that right now."

"What about Spencer? I'm sure he keeps you busy."

"He's pretty self-sufficient. I need something to keep my mind busy."

Hope sighed and set her cup down on the nearby table. She sat silent before speaking. "Well, if you must know, yes. I've been hearing some things are going missing. Mainly jewelry. It hasn't been enough for anyone to think it's not people simply forgetting where they put things or that it's just a case of losing it themselves. But I've been overhearing things like that more and more in the shop."

Anne rapped on the table with her knuckles. "Thankfully, nothing like that has happened at the inn."

"You're right. Nothing there." She picked her cup up again and took a sip. "Sorry, I don't think it's anything. Except—"

Anne leaned forward in her chair. "Except what?"

"No. Nothing."

"Come on. What?"

"I noticed that some jewelry has gone missing in the shop. It was in the display case up front so I'm not sure how anyone could have gotten into it. I haven't seen the items listed on our sales spreadsheet. They weren't super expensive, but they were actual gemstones, so they did hold some value."

"When did you notice this?"

"A while back. Probably a month or so."

"Maybe they were trying out what they planned to do earlier before the busy holiday season. When there are a lot of people around it's much easier to pocket things, but a test run could make it even easier." Anne stood. "Thanks for the tea. I've got to run."

"Okay, happy hunting." Anne

ignored the smirk on Hope's face.

Chapter Four

Anne decided the best course of action was to go straight to the source. She could pop into Jay's Jewelry and act like she needed to talk with Maggie about some of the town's Christmas decoration plans.

She dressed in a long-sleeved shirt before adding a vest to her ensemble. While she never got the point of a vest before, it was much easier to stash her phone and other items in the many vest pockets and not have to worry about carrying a purse. Plus, this time of year was crazy with temperature changes. It could be cold and snowing in the morning, then warm and sunny in the afternoon. She looked at the weather gauge—forty degrees. Yep, the vest would be enough.

Anne felt a brush against her legs and bent down to pick up the cat. "Now, Mouser, I just fed you and you know you can't go with me. Why don't you head upstairs as I bet that bird will be outside on that branch about now." She brushed her hand down his back and set him back down before stepping outside.

A storm had passed through a few days ago, and heaps of snow still dotted the landscape like fondant. As she lifted her chin toward the heavens she was once again enchanted with the cerulean blue sky with nary a cloud in sight. She took in a deep breath of the crisp mountain air and started off toward the trail that led into town.

Anne was glad she'd decided on wearing her snow boots with the slip-resistant soles as there were still some spots that had snow in heaps that could be icy. She listened to the quiet which had become such a calming influence after she'd moved to Carolan Springs. A couple of women walked past her with a golden lab. They took a moment to say hello and for the lab to garner some quick pets from her.

Arriving at the trailhead, she made her way across the main

avenue toward the street that would take her to the jewelry shop. She entered the shop to see Maggie at the counter helping a young couple look at engagement rings. Maggie waved at Anne who walked over to a case that held a display of earrings and necklaces.

"Can I help you?" The deep male voice intoned.

Anne jumped. "Oh, sorry. You startled me." She looked at the man who wore an expensive navy suit and a gold tie with a dark sapphire tie-pin.

He grinned and Anne noted what appeared to be a bright white set of veneers. He would have fit right at home in someplace like New York, LA or even possibly Aspen, but he stuck out like a sore thumb here in Carolan Springs. "Sorry, I didn't mean to scare you. I'm Jayson."

She glanced at his nametag, "Oh, I didn't know Jay had a son."

He laughed heartily. "No, Jayson. Not Jay's son. We're not related. I only work here."

Anne blushed at the gaff.

"Sorry, I—"

"It's fine. Now, what can I show you? Those emerald filagree earrings would look great on you."

Swarmy, that was it. Anne stared at him for a minute. "I'm just waiting for Maggie to be done. I need to talk to her."

The smile left his face for a brief moment, but he quickly recovered. "While you're waiting, why not try on one of these bracelets?" He pulled a set out from the case and Anne couldn't help herself as she pointed to one like Maggie had worn the other day.

"Excellent choice." He took out a cloth and gave it a polish before opening the clasp and fitting it on Anne's wrist.

"It's beautiful." Anne turned her wrist back and forth watching the embedded rubies glimmer with the light.

"Why don't I wrap it up for you?" He smiled broadly.

"Um, no. But thanks." She reluctantly removed the bracelet

from her wrist. "I'm really here to speak with Maggie."

"About?" He polished the bracelet and returned it to the display.

"Well ..." She decided it might be good to question him too. "Have you been hearing about the jewelry robberies?"

"What!" He apologized when the couple turned at his outburst. Lowering his voice, he continued, "I don't know. Should we be worried? Do we need to beef up our security? This is a busy time of the year for us.”

“From what I understand, it’s more to do with things going missing in hotels, inns, that type of place. Also, some stores have noticed small things missing. Not anything big though.”

He breathed deeply. “Good. Our sales are critical for—” He stopped as a man had entered the shop, “If you will excuse me, I should see how I can help him.”

Anne nodded, “Sure. I think Maggie may be done soon.”

The couple exited the store and Maggie signaled for Anne to come over. "Hello. Are you here about the bracelet? I can certainly give you a discount on it."

Anne hesitated. She did like that bracelet. "Um, let me think about it. No, I'm here because of the robberies that are starting to happen around the area and was wondering if you had heard anything about it. However, it sounds like Jayson didn't know about them."

"I think we should be okay.

We're careful about locking the jewelry up at night in the back and really this town is pretty safe. However, if you think it's important, I could talk to Jayson about sending out an email to our clients to be safe as we move into the holiday season."

"That might be a good idea. If you think of anything else or you have any ideas for the town's decorations, you can give me a call or drop by my house for a cup of coffee. I live next door to the Brandywine Inn."

Maggie looked up as a couple of women came in the door. "I may take you up on that, but I'll need to wait on them for now."

"Sure. Thanks."

"Not at all." She bent down and whispered, "And don't forget the discount offer."

Anne waved goodbye to Maggie as she left the shop. Where to now? As much as she hated the idea of talking to Sorcha, she knew that the bookstore and library was a hub of the town's activity. If anyone had heard anything about what was going on, she'd know.

She walked back up the hill toward the main street and stood for a moment as the hustle and bustle of the town happened around her. Crews had already begun hanging lights on the trees and a winter wonderland would be happening soon. They really had gotten a late start with their additions to the normal decorations. She waited until a car passed before crossing the street and making her way down toward the bookstore. Along the way she greeted others and she was reminded once again of the wonderful atmosphere of the town's residents which—knock on wood—seemed to rub off on visitors as well.

Anne stopped and admired the display Molly had done in the bookstore's windows. She'd created a wonderful scene, using open books to create artwork with it looking like the stories were coming to life from the pages of the books. She entered the store and was met with a wonderful smell of cinnamon and cider.

Molly popped up from where she'd been bending down behind the counter. "Hello, Ms. Freemont. How can I help you?"

"Hi Molly. I'm wondering if your mother is around."

"She's out on an errand, but she should be coming back soon if you want to wait a bit. There's hot apple cider over on the table with some butter cookies."

"Thanks, I'll take you up on the cider." Anne made her way to the cider and noticed a couple of women that were in deep conversation. She thought she recognized them from somewhere but couldn't place them. "Ladies."

They nodded at her and continued their chat. Anne took up a punchbowl style cup and ladled in some cider. She took a tentative sip of the hot cider and enjoyed the wonderful warmth that enveloped her.

Chapter Five

Anne strolled around the store and took in the various books. She stopped in front of the backyard farming area and saw that Molly had placed her book front and center with a big sign, "Local Author." Anne had come so far since those days of getting involved in growing her own food. She had a big yard now and had been plotting where to create a food forest. Even in the Colorado mountains and with the short season, you could still grow edible and medicinal herbs along with other plants.

She came around the corner and could barely see the two women bent toward one another. One of the woman's voices carried towards her. "I know that someone took my emerald ring."

"Maybe you mislaid it?"

Anne moved closer, but the women eyed her warily. She moved away and acted like she was looking at the bookshelf.

The woman spoke again. "No. I had taken it off to wash my hands. I went to dry my hands and when I turned back it was gone."

"Maybe it fell down the drain?" The other woman's voice carried over. Anne stifled a chuckle. The women could think they were being quiet, but the stage-whisper was so clear, it was as if she'd been standing next to them.

"No. I know someone took it." Her voice was adamant.

"Who could have done it, Susan?" Anne stole a glance

toward the women who continued talking unaware of anyone else.

"I don't know. It had to have been a woman, obviously."

Obviously? Anne's mind went back over the conversation. Ah, washing hands, women's bathroom ... But where?

"True. But wouldn't you have known who did it?"

"No. There were quite a few women in there. I didn't see anyone come near that sink. It was like a ghost came and swiped it from the shelf."

"Susan, I think you need to go to the police."

"I agree. I'd have gone back and looked, but the theater was closing."

Ah, the theater. Anne thought about the bathroom at the movie theater. She didn't recall any shelving over the sinks. She took another sip of her cider. Maybe she should check it out.

Although what was more interesting was that they

suspected a woman. While it hadn't occurred to her that it could be a woman, it made more sense. Women like to wander around shops, and even in a guesthouse, no one would think anything of them. In fact, it would be easy to look like you're one of the maids simply by holding some towels. No one would think twice about letting you into your room. She needed to make everyone at the inn aware just in case that was how the woman was stealing the jewelry. Talk about bold. So, it had to be someone who—Anne squealed as a hand touched her arm.

"I heard you were looking for me?" It was Sorcha. She made no apology for startling Anne.

"Um, yes. Is there somewhere we can talk in private?" She didn't want Susan and her friend to overhear their conversation.

"Sure. Follow me." Sorcha sashayed past the women who kept their heads down toward the table.

Anne couldn't quite place them, but they looked so familiar. Maybe it would come to her later.

They reached the back and Sorcha turned towards her. When Anne had arrived in Carolan Springs, the pair had hit it off. That was until Anne had started taking up more of Sheriff Carson's time. Now they were formally cordial. Today Anne felt a bit more presentable than the first time they had met. Sorcha, however, still looked stunning with her burgundy and rust plaid shirtdress cinched by a large chocolate belt which only accentuated her womanly curves. She folded her arms in front of her and waited.

"Listen, I've been hearing about some robberies in town of jewelry. Since lots of people come in the bookstore and library, I was wondering if you'd heard anything.

"No. I haven't." She tucked a wayward strand of hair back up into the messy topknot.

"Okay, well, um ..."

"I have a lot of work to do. Is there anything else?"

Anne shook her head and Sorcha flounced off. She hated that she'd made an enemy of Sorcha. She needed to figure out some way to make their relationship better. Handing the cup to Molly, she made her way to the front of the store. The table where the ladies had been sitting was now empty. Although as she passed it, she noticed a crumpled piece of napkin with names written on it. She looked over her shoulder to make sure that Molly and Sorcha weren't watching before she scooped up the napkin. A list of possible suspects could be just the thing she needed.

Chapter Six

Anne arrived home to find a note from Spencer saying he'd be home later and not to worry about dinner as he was catching a pizza and movie with friends.

Hm, a movie. Theater. That's what one of those women had said at the bookstore. It was still early so Anne popped over to the inn. Everything was running smoothly so she returned home just as her phone rang. It was an unknown number. Normally she wouldn't answer, but it could be important.

"Hello?" She put the phone on speaker and laid it on the counter before shrugging out of one arm of her vest.

A woman's voice came over the line. "Hello. Is this Anne? This is Maggie."

Anne slipped the vest off completely before picking up the phone. "Hi Maggie. What's up?"

"I forgot to tell you something, well, is it okay, if I come over to your place? I think it's a bit more private."

"Sure. I'm home right now. I'll put some coffee on unless you prefer tea." Anne gave her the address.

"Coffee sounds great. Be there soon." The call disconnected. Anne busied herself with scooping the coffee beans from the jar and placing them into the grinder. Kandi must have stopped by as she spied cranberry chocolate cookies on a plate when she went to pour fresh water in the pot.

"Yum. These will go perfect with coffee."

Since Maggie would be arriving soon, Anne took some time to stash the Christmas boxes in the back room. Thankfully, she'd stopped Kandi from putting up all of the main Christmas decorations over at the inn. After much pouting on Kandi's part, they'd agreed that lights could go up and the tree situated. However, that the entry, dining, and main staircase had to be focused on Thanksgiving until December.

Kandi had taken that and run with it so now the inn's tree was decorated in golds, and browns, along with cornucopias adorning the tables. At this rate, she wouldn't be surprised if Kandi pressed to leave it up until Valentine's. Oh well, it made her and the guests happy so that's all that mattered.

Even though the day had warmed, the room felt a bit chilly. Anne started a fire in the fireplace, and it had begun to warm the living room when the doorbell rang.

"Come in." Anne held back the door and beckoned Maggie inside.

Maggie had on a light blue jacket and removed it as she came into the room. "Oh, nice. With the sun it's a bit deceiving out there. Looks warm, but it's pretty nippy. Do you mind?" She nodded toward the fireplace.

"Not at all. We can pull our chairs closer to the fire while we enjoy our coffee. What do you take?"

"Just cream, please."

"I can do that. Back in a jiff." As Anne returned with the coffee, Maggie warmed her hands in front of the fire. Anne set the two cups of coffee down on a walnut tray along with a small plate of cookies and napkins.

"Here we are." She took the seat opposite Maggie. "So, Maggie, have you lived here long?"

Maggie took a sip of the brew and shook her head. "No, I went to college in Denver and decided I liked it here. I was looking for a job and this one showed up. I interviewed and here I am."

"So, you've been here …"

"About five months now. I want to see if I can handle the winters. Where I come from we don't get lots of snow, if any at all, so seeing if this works for me."

"I have to say, this isn't normally where I'd find a younger person moving. I love it, but there's not a lot going on. You'd probably have to go to Denver for much entertainment."

"I'm an introvert so that doesn't bother me at all. I prefer a smaller, quieter place." She set her cup down. "That's kind of why I'm here. I thought that this place should be safe. But if there's robberies going on ... well, that's a bit scary."

"Oh, don't worry. We'll figure it out."

Maggie picked up one of the cookies and broke off a piece before popping it in her mouth. "Oh, those are good. So much for my diet." She dusted her fingertips on a napkin. "If you don't mind me asking, what do you mean we'll figure it out?"

"Well, not to brag, but we've had a few mysteries in this town, and I've helped solve them. I know we can solve this one too."

"Really? Well, that's interesting. How do you plan to do it? Maybe I can help."

Anne held her cup with both hands, "Thanks. I have to think about it and then things just start to line up."

"You mean, the clues reveal themselves or the solution?"

"I guess you could say both." Anne placed her cup on the table. "Things just come together at some point."

Maggie uncrossed her legs and smoothed down her navy slacks, each pant leg fashioned with a sharp crease. "Okay. I feel a bit better then. I know Jayson was upset about what you'd said. I think he's really struggling right now. Business hasn't been exactly booming and the inventory is a bit expensive for what I think this town may be able to afford."

"Interesting. Since you're here, how much was the diamond and gold bracelet you were wearing the other night?"

Maggie smiled. "Ten thousand."

Anne sputtered and coughed as she swallowed her coffee. "I'm sorry. I thought you said ten thousand."

Maggie's laughter made Anne smile back at the woman. "See,

exactly. Who can afford that kind of thing here? He should have set up shop in Aspen or Cherry Creek."

"How much was the ring you were wearing, if you don't mind me asking?"

"Hold on to your chair ... Fifty-thousand."

Anne sat forward in her chair. "Oh, wow. I can't imagine."

"You can't imagine? I fiddled with that ring all night, I was so worried it would fall off somewhere. As soon as I left the house and got in my car, I put it right back in its box."

"Isn't Jayson worried that something could happen to the jewelry?"

Maggie crossed her legs and set her unadorned hands in her lap. "He's insured. All the jewelry in the shop is. You have to be since the jewelry inventory is essential to the shop."

She stood. "Well, I don't know if I feel much better knowing there still may be someone out there robbing people. Though if nothing else, I'm glad I had a chance to chat with you more." She walked over to the door and slid her arms into the jacket. "Thanks for letting me stop by."

"Of course. I'm glad to meet more people in town. I haven't been here all that long either." Anne opened the front door.

"Well, goodbye. Good luck on your sleuthing." She waved as she moved off the porch and down to where an older model Subaru was parked.

Anne returned the wave. "Well, she's got the quintessential Colorado car at least." She closed and locked the front door before returning to the pie-table between the chairs. She picked up the tray and returned it to the kitchen. Pouring herself another cup of coffee, she decided to sit by the fire. First she needed to look at that list of names. She pulled the folded napkin from her vest that she retrieved from the kitchen and made her way to the chair. Setting her coffee cup on the table, she set the napkin down beside it before stoking the fire. It roared into life and the warmth again penetrated into the room.

Anne sat down and taking the napkin, unfolded it. There was a list of five names on the list, but one stood out from the rest.

Chapter Seven

"Seriously!" Anne laughed. Her name was third on the list. "Well, I can definitely scratch one name off the list." She looked at the other names. They were names she didn't recognize—except one. Margaret Hanson.

Anne stared into the fire. Had Margaret—Maggie—come by to see what information she could get out of Anne? She would be the last person Anne would consider, but isn't that always the way it turns out? Someone you don't suspect. It did make sense if the robberies had started in the last few months. Maybe she'd been trying out her plan on smaller fish before she—wait, did Maggie plan to steal from the jewelry store? No, suspicion would immediately fall on staff. No, that can't be it. Anne gazed into the fire, but no insights popped into her brain.

"Hmmm, what to do now?" She retrieved her phone and dialed Kandi's number.

"Hi, ya. What's up?"

"I overheard some ladies talking about a ring being stolen at the theater. I'm going to head over there. Scope out the bathroom and find out what I can. However, everyone else has stuff to do for decoration committee, what do you want me to do? I figure I can run some errands while I'm out too."

"Good idea. Um, how about asking merchants if they'll do a little present for people who come into their shops?"

"I can do that. That could get expensive though."

"Good point. How about a one-day event? It could finish with the tree lighting in the evening."

"That could work." Anne walked over and pulled a notepad and pen from her desk. "What day are you thinking?"

"How about, like, the Saturday after Thanksgiving?"

"Let me stop by the shops and see what they think. Just Main Street shops?"

"Yes. Anyone can do it. I just hope we solve the mystery of the thief before then."

"Me too. I had a conversation with Maggie just a bit ago." Anne banked the fire so the coals would stay hot and ready for a fire in the evening while she was out.

"Oh. What'd she say?"

"Not much. She's worried about the robberies."

"Me too. Anything else?"

"Well, when I was at Sorcha's-- those two ladies who were talking

…"

"Yes?"

Anne placed the fire poker back on its stand and picked up her cup. "You know, they looked familiar, but I couldn't place them."

"You know how it is. That happens lots of times."

"I guess. Anyway, they left a napkin with names on it. I picked it up and that gives me an idea of who was at the theater when they were there."

"Cool. I thought you'd get it."

Anne rinsed out her cup, "What?"

Kandi cleared her throat, "You know. Solve the crime. You've got a great mind, that's all."

"Well, I can mark one off the list as it's me. I haven't been to the movies in a while though. But one was more interesting. They had Maggie's name on there."

"Really. That is interesting. But I can't see her doing something—"

Anne continued, "And they were talking about going to the

police. I think I may go talk to Deputy—"

"No!" Kandi squealed over the phone.

"What in the world?"

"Think about it. If you, like, go to the police, it's bound to get out that someone's on to them. We can't do that." The phone went silent. "Plus, Carson will be coming back soon, and you can talk to him about it on the down-low."

"How do you know Carson is

coming back soon? He hasn't said anything to me in our conversations." Anne hit speaker before sitting the phone on the counter so she could wipe her hands and grab her coat.

"I just figure that he'll be back for the holidays, that's all."

"Um, okay." Anne checked her coat pockets to ensure she had gloves and a hat in case the weather turned.

Kandi chirped, "Listen, I have to go. Let me know how you get on with the store vendors. I think it would make a fun day for the town.”

“Okay. See you later.” Anne disconnected the call. “Hmm, where to first?” She decided it would be a good time to check out the theater. She pulled her keys from the rack by the back door and went out to the enclosed porch where she slipped out of her house shoes and back into boots. As she pulled them on, she heard the sound of receiving a text on her phone.

She looked down. It was from

Maggie. "I think I may know something."

Chapter Eight

Anne typed back. "What?," but no response came back. She probably had a customer come in. She could talk to her later. For now, Anne could check out the theater and visit the shops. Anne called up Stanley and asked if he'd like to tag along. He agreed and soon the pair were parking at the end of Main Street.

"Do you want to go together or split up?"

"Let's each take a side of the street. Then we can meet up at the café when we're done. I could go for some chicken-fried steak and gravy with biscuits." The elderly gentleman rubbed his hands together and grinned.

"Why Stanley, are you asking me out on a date? Whatever would Velma think?" She batted her eyes and spoke with a long southern drawl.

"She's at her sister's this week. A man's gotta eat. And what's better than having a beautiful young woman as your dining companion?" He winked.

"Stanley, flattery will get you everywhere. I'm game and I love their tortilla soup. Here." She handed Stanley a stack of simple flyers she'd made before about the committee's idea with the presence theme. He saluted and sauntered off across the street.

Anne knew that Stanley would move fast to get to the café, so she set out on her side of the street. Making her way down the block, she was encouraged when the shop owners loved the theme idea and the tiny presents for shoppers. Anne walked down the street and paused as a thought came to her. Not a movie theater, but the playhouse. She glanced over to see where Stanley was in his efforts. He was behind her at a store with Colorado items and was in conversation with the manager. She knew that when those two got together they could talk for hours. She could pop over to the theater and finish these later if she needed to.

She set off at a fast pace and cut down the alley connection next to Hope's Herbal Shoppe. From there it was only another block before she made it to the old schoolhouse that had been converted into a local playhouse and community hub with an outdoor garden for free community concerts and a couple of restaurants. Now if only the theater was open. It wasn't a day for matinees and the next opening for their Christmas performance wasn't scheduled for at least a couple of weeks. She remembered a side door used by crew to take food in the back way. She'd have a better chance entering from there and avoid prying eyes.

Slipping in the side door, she wound her way past the entrance to the wing which housed the bathrooms. She opened the door and flipped on the overhead light. This area held a couch and mirrors, Anne moved past it to open the door where the sinks were located. She opened the door and as she faced the mirrors, she gasped.

On the mirror in bright red lipstick were the words, "BACK OFF OR ELSE!"

A bang outside caused her to yell out. Was it the robber? Anne rushed out of the bathroom toward the lobby. A door was swinging from someone's abrupt exit. She sprinted toward it. Carefully opening the door, she caught her breath.

No one was there.

The long hall stretched ahead,

and they must have gone into one of the other doors. Unfortunately, once they were in the main part of the school she wouldn't be able to tell who had been in here. She sprinted over to the closest door, but something on the floor caught her eye. It was a scarf—light blue with silver threads and stars. Anne picked it up. Whoever had been coming after her had made their first mistake. She shoved it into her pocket and opened the door to the busy goings-on of the main hallway. After scanning the crowd, she saw no one that looked to be the owner of the scarf. Anne glanced at her wristwatch. She needed to get back and meet up with Stanley. However, she needed to preserve the proof.

Anne ran back in and took a photo of the mirror. Looking at the bathroom more would have to wait, but maybe she could gain some insight from the photo.

Chapter Nine

After enjoying a nice meal with Stanley, Anne finished up taking the flyers to the rest of the shops. She drove Stanley home and gave him a peck on the cheek before he exited the vehicle. She needed to talk with Kandi or Hope. As luck would have it, Hope had been checking in at the Brandywine Inn, so she invited Kandi and Hope over for a cup of tea.

"What do you think?" Anne

broached the subject.

Hope perched on the edge of a kitchen chair. "Can we see all the clues you have?"

Anne went into the living room and returned with the napkin. "Okay, so here's what I have so far."

She placed a sheet of paper on the table. "First, jewelry is going missing. Two, Maggie is new to town and works at the jewelry store. Three, two women were talking, and one says that their ring was taken at the theater. They wrote down five names on this napkin."

Hope looked at it. "I gotta go with this one. She's most likely the culprit." She pointed at Anne's name.

"Ha ha." Anne responded. "Then today, a message on the theater mirror." She showed them the picture on her phone. "This means someone knows that I'm looking for clues."

Kandi giggled and Hope shot her a look. "This isn't funny, Kandi. Someone is getting nervous."

Anne responded, "Kandi tends to giggle all the time, but does it when she's anxious too."

"That's right!" Kandi responded. "I'm, like, worried, that's all."

Kandi and Hope exchanged looks with each other before Kandi stuck out her tongue.

Anne stood and went over to where her coat hung on the hook by the door. "Whoever was in the theater with me, dropped this."

She set the scarf down on the table.

"Who do you think it is? That list is only who they think did it. It could very well be someone who's not on that list." Hope stood and paced the room.

"I thought of that too. I'm really wondering about Maggie being on that list. Doesn't that seem weird to you? I didn't know her, but they did."

Kandi scanned the items on the table. "Hm, so let's think here. Jewelry, jewelry store, I don't know. Nothing is coming to me." She sat back and crossed her arms.

"Maybe Maggie is doing this, because she's getting ready to rob Jay's store for a real profit?"

"I don't know. I don't think—" Kandi glanced over at Hope.

"I agree. We don't want to falsely accuse someone. She could lose her job."

Anne looked at the pair. "Why is it I feel like you two are keeping something from me?"

"Why do you say that?" They responded in unison.

"That!" Anne retorted. "It's the second time now. Kandi, first you and Stewart and now you and Hope."

Hope perched on the chair, "We're not. But I don't want to go making accusations that could cause someone harm either. Do you?"

"No. Of course not." She leaned back against the counter.

Kandi pushed a lock of hair

behind her ear and cocked her head. "How about I go by tomorrow and talk to them about the little presents thing? I could see what I think of Maggie and report back."

Anne sat back in her chair. "That's an idea. Sure."

"And now for some not-so-good news." Hope grasped the back of a chair.

"What?" Anne took a sip of her wine.

"Turns out that Callie is

quitting. That means we'll have to cover the inn between us for the next few weeks."

"Hope, I know you're busy at the shop. Kandi and I can handle it."

Kandi popped up, "Well, this isn't good. I was supposed to help Polly with getting the stores to figure out their decorations and set up the boxes around town for the snow-globe pictures."

"I guess I could ask Spencer to help out."

"I've already nabbed him and Stewart to do the heavy lifting."

Anne sighed, "Great. That means it looks like I'll be stuck here then. That will put finding anything else out at a full stop."

"We can still help out once we've got everything in place. But I think for now you should step back anyway—especially after that message. I don't want anything bad to happen to you." Kandi answered Anne.

"Okay. Let me see if I can figure it out without going anywhere."

She pointed to Kandi, "But as soon as you talk to Maggie, you let me know."

"I will."

Chapter Ten

The next weeks flew by and Anne kept busy with the comings and goings of the Brandywine Inn. In her spare time, she hounded Kandi for news of any more robberies or if she'd spoken to Maggie. They'd looked into Maggie's text and followed that lead, but it had turned into a dead-end.

Kandi shared with Anne that Maggie had an idea of a delivery driver being the thief. They could access lots of places and no one would even think twice about them. It had been a good idea, but most of the drivers were long-time residents and male. The woman in the theater had noted it was a woman.

Was there more than one person stealing jewelry? It could be a possibility. Anne was itching to get back to her own sleuthing, but their business had to take precedence.

Kandi came over in the evening

and after much cajoling convinced Anne that she'd get more into the Christmas spirit if she'd put up her decorations. They decided to have a tree-trimming party and invited Molly, Hope, and Eliza. Spencer and Molly set to work on decorating the tree while Stewart took charge of hanging garland and lighting. Eliza and Hope unwrapped the various ornaments while Kandi bounced from group to group, enjoying the moment. Finally, the decorations were complete.

Anne picked up a mug of hot chocolate and rose it in the air. "Thank you everyone for helping me decorate and for being the best people I know."

Others toasted with their drinks. Anne had just set down her cup when a flash of black rushed past her. "No Mouser!" She tried to grab at the cat, but he was too fast for her. Spencer and Molly made a dash, but the cat had already attacked the tree. Ornaments scattered everywhere as they all tried to catch them before they fell to the ground and broke.

"Ack. I knew this was going to be an issue." Anne scooped up Mouser and took him back to the kitchen before shutting the large oak door between the rooms. "I guess that's one of the reasons they needed doors back in the early days. Not just to hide the help in the kitchen area, but to keep pesky critters from getting into things."

Kandi reached down and picked up an ornament. It was an

older ornament that had a metal cap on top which held the hook for hanging on the tree. When Mouser had shot toward the tree, this one had detached and fell into the branches.

"Hm, this one is missing that top part." Molly searched the tree until she found it. As she began to put the ornament back together, she said, "What's this?" She pointed the ornament's opening toward the group. "It's a piece of paper."

"Here, let me help." Eliza

opened a small box and pulled out tweezers. She handed them to Molly who carefully pulled a rolled up piece of paper from the ornament. She handed it over to Anne.

Anne unwrapped it and an exclamation escaped her lips. "This isn't just a piece of paper, it's a piece of my history."

Christmas 1959

The young woman set the baby down in the crib next to their bed. She surveyed the cramped room that held their double bed which was pushed up against a far wall, and the crib. They barely had room to walk, but she'd wanted to keep the living room nice in case any of the other private's wives stopped by. You normally didn't have a ready-made family as a private and she should be grateful that they'd been allowed a two-bedroom apartment for the other girls.

Vel busied herself in the kitchen, and sat down to gaze at the tiny, scrawny Christmas tree in the corner. The girls had helped decorate it so most of the silver tinsel had ended up in big clumps near the bottom. At night when they'd gone to bed, she'd tried to spread it out some, but had been so tired by the end of the day that she'd finally given up. She stared at the presents underneath the tree. Between the girls and Santa, she knew every present.

She'd finally given in to her emotions and Herb had caught her crying.

"What's the matter?" He took her in his arms.

"It's the first time in my life that I know what every single present contains under the tree." She felt bad because it wasn't like you could get a raise as an enlisted private. She knew that the other mothers had confided that they were struggling financially as well.

"I'm sorry."

"Don't be sorry. You know I love you." He kissed her forehead.

"I love you too." She wiped the tears from her eyes.

Before long, it was Christmas

Eve. They'd decided to open their presents in the evening and then Santa would come overnight. When they were with extended family, they'd open other presents.

She sat and watched as the girls opened their presents.

"Okay, girls. That's it. We need to get you into the bath and to bed so Santa can come."

The older girl just rolled her eyes but picked up the youngest, placing her on her hip.

"Wait, I think there's another present." Herb remarked.

"No, that's all of them." Vel replied.

"Go, look." He grinned.

With his encouragement, she went to the back of the tree and hidden deep in the back branches was a wrapped package. The tag read: *Love, From Mr. Magoo.*

She turned to him. "What?"

"No one should go without at least one present that's a surprise to them."

She unwrapped the present which contained two frilly aprons. Tears sprung to her eyes. "But how?"

"It's nothing. Who needs lunch anyway?" He winked.

She flung her arms around his neck. "Thank you."

"Don't thank me. I just want to know why Mr. Magoo is sending you presents."

***

"Ah, that's so sweet. So, they were ..."

"My grandparents. My mother said that every year, my grandmother got a present from Mr. Magoo. Sometimes it was hidden on the tree or somewhere else with some clues. She said the saddest Christmas was when there were no gifts to hunt for from Mr. Magoo."

Kandi chirped, "Who's Mr. Magoo?"

"He was a bungling cartoon character who was always having problems, because he couldn't see well."

Eliza wiped her tweezers and placed them back in the box before putting them away in her purse. "This is such a wonderful story that is full of good memories."

"Yes."

"Tell us. What does this note say?"

Anne read the yellowed note: *"Sardines my dear, were not in my plan, but I'll give you your present if you'll hold out your hand. All my love, Herb."*

Kandi came over and looked at the note. "I wonder what the gift was that year."

"If I recall correctly, it was a diamond ring. He'd wrapped a tin of sardines and of course, when you shake that, it made it difficult to guess what the present held. "

Anne folded the note back up and tucked it back inside the ornament before returning it to a protected spot on the tree.

She smiled as her heart felt the tug of the memory of love and sacrifice.

Chapter Eleven

"That's such a neat story. Thanks for sharing it. I told my mom I'd be home soon, so I need to get going." Molly added.

After goodbyes and hugs, Spencer left with Stewart to drive Molly home. Eliza, Kandi, and Hope sat at the kitchen table chatting. Finally, Anne spoke, "I hate that I haven't been able to make any progress on the robberies. Any news there?"

Hope responded, " A few storeowners have had some break-in's."

"Really?" Kandi questioned.

"No. Really, Kandi." Hope shot Kandi a look.

Kandi's eyes grew wide. "Wow. Well, that's …"

"That's what?" Anne intoned. "I feel like you all are leaving me in the dark on something."

Eliza interjected, "Dearest Anne. You know that your friends only want the best for you."

"Yes. I guess ..." Anne looked at each of them, who nodded at Eliza's statement. "Fine. Have you been over to talk with Maggie again?"

"I stopped by. She couldn't talk for long. Only mentioned that she had some suspicions, but nothing firm."

"Okay, well, what about the other women on the list?"

Kandi slipped off her shoes and tucked her feet under her in the chair. "I looked into them. One has moved away so she's out of the picture." She starred at Anne. "You want to confess?"

"Ha ha. No." Anne folded her hands in her lap.

"Okay, then that narrows it down. One works at the theater, one I'm still looking for, and Maggie. I can't see Maggie doing anything like this though." Kandi picked up the Christmas-themed cups and started washing them.

Anne came over and dried the cups before stating, "I think I should go speak to Maggie. I can make up something about looking at the bracelet or looking for a gift."

"I guess that would be all right." Kandi shot a look toward Hope who nodded.

"What's up with you two?"

"We just want to make sure you don't get in over your head. That warning means that they may be feeling threatened by you."

"Okay, I'll be safe. I promise." She held up her fingers in a scout's honor pose. Everyone had left for home when Anne's cellphone rang. She looked down at the caller ID, Carson. She smiled.

"Hello you."

"Hello back to you. Miss me?"

She normally would have hemmed and hawed, but she was done with pretending. "Yes, I've missed you. When are you coming home?"

"I'll be back this Sunday. How's everyone doing?"

"We're all fine. We put the tree up tonight and the house looks so pretty. The offer to stay here is open you know."

"Yes, but I don't think that's wise. Especially with an impressionable teenager in the house. I bought a used travel-trailer here and I plan on putting it out on my property. Then I can oversee the reconstruction of the house."

Anne tried to hide her disappointment. Carson's home had been burned down and it made sense that a new structure should be built there.

He continued, "So, anything

else going on while I'm away?"

"Um ..."

"That tells me everything I need to know. What are you involved in now?"

Anne shared about the local robberies and the names on the list, but she left out the warning on the bathroom mirror.

"It figures. How about this? I'll check in with Deputy Ruiz just to get his take on everything. Would that make you happy?"

"Yes. I said I'd go talk to him,

but Kandi said it would warn the robber off."

"She's right. They won't know if I contact him. Now, try not to get into any more trouble before I get back, okay?"

"You know me."

"Yes, which is why I'm asking for your word."

"Fine." She twirled a lock of hair between her fingers. "Till Sunday."

"Till Sunday." The call ended.

That was in a few days. She

really wished he'd be back for the tree-lighting, but there was nothing she could do about it. She needed to talk to Maggie and see if she could make any headway before Carson came back.

Mouser did a looping circle in a figure eight around her legs. Anne picked him up. "Mouser, I bet you could catch the thief right away if only you were human." The cat gave a loud 'meow.'

"Agreed."

Chapter Twelve

The next morning Anne woke to softly falling snow. She dressed warmly before heading over to the jewelry store. Maggie had said she'd known something, maybe Anne could coax it out of her. Tomorrow there'd be lots of people arriving to town for the Main Street event and the tree lighting. They would need to stop the thief, or the robberies could give the town a bad reputation. Not to mention the fact that the crimes could escalate, and someone could get hurt.

Driving through the streets, she saw people putting the finishing touches on various decorations. The store fronts were festive and decked out in various fun facades of presents with ribbons and bows.

Stanley's idea of a snow-globe for taking pictures had been met with lots of enthusiasm. The decorating committee had built large boxes on both ends of Main Street, one close to the tree on the square and another one that was more hidden and known only to locals which had been located down by the lake. That one had the back left open, because of the backdrop of snow-capped mountains overlooking a lake. Families or couples could hike or snowshoe down to the lake and take pictures before hiking back into town.

Anne parked her car in front of the jewelry store. She gathered her bag and thought through what she was going to say to Maggie. Inside, she was met by someone she hadn't seen before.

The woman greeted her. "Hello, may I help you?"

"I'm looking for Maggie. Is she in?"

"Who?" The woman had a puzzled look on her face.

"Maggie." Anne repeated.

"I'll handle this, Robin." Jayson waited until the woman had left before he took Anne's arm and moved toward a corner.

Anne shook free from his grasp.

"I'm looking for Maggie."

"Aren't we all. I only know this. She told me she was visiting her aunt and wouldn't be in over the weekend. She knows this is going to be a busy time at our shop. I had to hire in someone from Denver and let me tell you, it's costing me a lot of money for her stunt."

Anne shook her head, "That doesn't seem like Maggie. I can't see here just leaving like that."

"Do you know her that well then?"

"Actually no, not really."

"All I know is that I'm going to be swamped and she's left me in the lurch. She has no job when she gets back." He looked toward the cases. "Now, unless you need some help picking out jewelry, I've got lots to do before tomorrow."

Anne waved him away, "No. Thanks." She left the store and sat in her car. Was Maggie the robber after all? She still had no proof, but why take off right before the biggest sales event of this month? It made sense that she would work on commission, so this was hurting her too. Anne drummed her fingers on the steering wheel. She should call Maggie first and get her side of the story.

Anne dialed the number, but it went direct to voicemail. "Maggie, it's Anne. Can you give me a call please?" She started up her car and pulled into traffic. On the way back, she spotted Kandi's bright red truck at the diner. She pulled into a vacant spot and made her way inside. Kandi was sitting at a table with a woman Anne didn't know. They looked up and Kandi said something to the woman who rose from the table and headed to the doors in the back.

"Hi. Who was that?" Anne slid into the booth.

"Who?" Kandi fiddled with a piece of rye toast.

"That woman you were just talking to." Anne waited while the waitress handed her a menu. Instead of looking through it, Anne replied that she'd have a western omelet with green chili on the side, and a hazelnut latte.

"Oh, her. She's helping out with the event tomorrow." Kandi took a bite of toast, stopping any further conversation.

The waitress brought Anne her coffee and removed the detritus left behind by the other woman. After wiping down the table, the waitress asked if there was anything else for right now and then departed when Anne replied, "No, thanks."

"Kandi, I went over to the jewelry shop to speak with Maggie."

"Un, huh. And?"

"She's gone."

Kandi's brow furrowed. "What do you mean she's gone?"

"She's left. Jayson told me that she told him she was visiting her aunt. She's left him in the lurch, what with the events happening tomorrow."

Kandi wiped her mouth with a napkin. "That doesn't sound like Maggie. If anything, she goes above and beyond on helping out. She did a lot with the event."

"In what way?"

"She took over going to visit all the shops and ..."

Their eyes met. "Oh, no. You don't think ..."

"That she was looking for the best places to hit?" Anne sighed. "I hate to say it, but maybe she's been playing us all along."

"I agree." Kandi sat back in the booth. "Looks like you've solved the case."

"What are you talking about? We need to find Maggie."

"We will."

A cold breeze came through the door and Anne turned to spy Hope scanning the diners. When she spied the pair, she came over and slid in next to Anne. "We have to do something."

"What do you mean?" Anne swiveled in her seat to get a better view of Hope.

"Maggie. She's not answering my calls."

"We know. We were just talking about it."

"Kandi, I called her aunt after I kept trying to get ahold of her. She had an appointment with me this week. Maggie had written her aunt's name and phone number as her contact. She hasn't heard from Maggie either. After her aunt couldn't reach her, she contacted the police so they could do a wellness check-in. No one where she lives has seen her for days."

Hope looked around before lowering her voice, "Maggie's missing."

Chapter Thirteen

Anne had tossed and turned all night trying to figure out what had happened to Maggie. Had she gone to ground so that she could pull off a robbery or just up and left? That option seemed out of character for the young woman.

The phone rang and she answered it. "Kandi, what's up? It's a bit early for your call."

"This is important. Last night the jewelry store was robbed."

"What?" Anne shot up in bed.

"Yes, I can't get much information, but Stewart overheard it on his scanner. It sounds like the person had to have known what pieces were the most valuable, but easy to sell. I hate to say it, but—"

"Oh, no ... I can't believe it. Maggie must have been planning this all along." She leaned against the headboard as Mouser hopped up next to her. "Well, there's not much we can do now. I think we'll have to leave it to the police."

"Agreed. On another subject, you're going to come with me to the tree lighting, right?"

"I don't know. I'm thinking of staying in—"

"You can't." Kandi yelped.

"It's just a tree-lighting. I'll see it lit up the entire month and more."

"You promised." Anne could imagine the pout on Kandi's face.

"Ugh, stab me in the heart. Fine." She stroked Mouser who had curled up next to her.

"Good. Stewart and I will pick you up—say six-ish?"

"Fine." Anne threw off the covers making Mouser jump from the bed. She stood and stretched.

"See you then." Kandi ended the call.

Anne spent the morning reminding guests that they would be shutting down the offices at the Inn for the day and to contact her by phone if anything were needed. The day passed quickly, and Anne took time in dressing nicely for the tree-lighting. She wished Carson would be with her that evening, but nothing she could do about it.

Kandi knocked on the front door and Anne laughed. The young woman wore the elf ears hat and was dressed in Waldo gear that made her look like a living candy-cane.

"You're going to freeze in that." She hugged her.

"These are insulated. See? Plus, once the festivities are over with the mayor, Stewart has my coat. I'll only be like this for a short while."

They drove over to the town and parked in the backlot of Hope's Herbal Shoppe. It was a good thing as all the parking on Main Street was full. The town was festive in mood, and it had snowed again, leaving a beautiful icing covering the trees and rooftops. The huge tree was displayed in the midst of the town center and had large ornaments of varying sizes from small to basketball size, up to large beach balls placed on it. A few were on the bottom, so it didn't look empty, but the base had been left open so that families and guests could place their ornaments on the tree. Some had already hooked their ornaments on the tree and pictures of smiling families, happy pets, and other photos adorned every space. The larger balls had business logos in gold printed on them. People milled around the tree and walked along the main street while carolers from the local church choir sang songs while dressed in Victorian-style finery.

The mayor spoke to the crowd

and Anne noticed he was wearing a red tie. It reminded her of her welcome to the town and her eyes grew misty as she remembered that first introduction to the people in the town. It was also the first time she'd met Carson. She returned her attention to the stage where Kandi was speaking. The mayor thanked Kandi for all her work and stepping in last minute with helping the town holiday planning. She was given a big round of applause with her face turning bright red. After the applause had died, she started the countdown for the tree lighting.

"Ten, nine, eight …" the crowd yelled. "One!" The tree lit up with beautiful lights just as Anne felt a tap on her shoulder. She turned to see that it was Carson. Without thinking she grabbed his neck and gave him a kiss full-on the lips, right there in front of God and everybody.

He laughed. "Nice to see you too!"

"I thought you weren't coming home until tomorrow."

"Here, come with me." He pulled her away from the crowd and down the trail that led toward her house. As they rounded a curve, she spied Eliza, Stewart, Kandi, Spencer, and Molly.

"What's going on here?" She looked from them back to Carson.

"You know that you drive me crazy with all your mystery-solving?"

"O ... kay. But what is—?"

"I knew from Kandi that you'd become a bit cranky—"

Anne shot a look at Kandi who shrugged her shoulders.

Carson continued, "I just knew that I wanted to do something special for this."

"For what?"

Carson got down on one knee and drew out a box. He opened it and inside was a beautiful ring. "Anne, will you marry me?"

She yelped. "Of course. Yes!"

He was slipping the ring on her finger when a commotion behind them caused them all to swivel toward the caller. Hope raced toward them, a look of fear on her face.

She ran toward Hope. "What's wrong?"

"It's Maggie. She's gone."

Kandi met them. "We don't have to pretend anymore. Carson's just proposed."

"No, Kandi." Hope was shaking.

Anne turned to Kandi, "What do you mean 'pretend'?"

"It was all for you. We wanted

to do something that would make you happy, so we made up the jewelry robberies. Those ladies you overheard—they work for the theater. They're actresses. We thought that we could have you figure out Carson's proposal, but I think the last part of it got missed by Maggie."

"You mean she was part of it too?"

Kandi nodded. "Yes, so it was a bit disappointing as she was supposed to call you into the shop to try on rings so Carson could ensure he had the one you wanted."

Hope shook her head. "That's the problem. Maggie had agreed to be part of it and keep Anne's focus on her, but she's really missing."

Chapter Fourteen

Carson moved toward Hope. "When was the last time you saw Maggie?"

"Um, let's see. About a week ago, I went into the jewelry shop. I told her that Anne figured things out quicker than we had anticipated and we needed to slow down her progress."

"Wait a minute!" Anne stepped forward. "So that's why I got hooked in to work at the Inn?"

"Yes. Callie didn't really quit. I just gave her time off since she wanted to visit her family."

Anne shook her finger at Kandi and Hope. "You, two!"

"We had to do something to keep you occupied so Carson could decide on his plan for proposing."

"Okay, I'll give you that. When's the last time you spoke with Maggie?"

Hope interjected, "A few days ago. She left a message on my

phone. She sounded rushed on the phone, but said she needed to talk to me right away. I tried calling back later, but she never returned the call." Hope ran her hands through her bob cut. "I didn't think anything of it. I know I've been swamped getting ready for today's traffic. But I stopped by her apartment and her next door neighbor hasn't seen her for days. She thought she'd gone out of town."

"Have you been to the jewelry store?"

"Yes, but they said they hadn't seen her either."

Anne paced around. "We need to go to the jewelry store."

"Why?" Carson responded.

"They had a break-in yesterday. Don't you find it odd that Maggie goes missing and then the store has a break-in? Maybe she realized this was her chance and took it." She looked at Carson. "Do you know if they're still processing the scene?"

"Possibly."

"Okay, then. What are we waiting for?" Anne rushed back into the crowd and the rest of the group followed her. Eliza waved them goodbye as she had plans to meet up with friends for dinner. Piling into Stewart's truck, they quickly made it to the jewelry shop. The front door had a closed sign on it next to a boarded up window. Lighting showed that people were inside.

"They're using the back entrance for now." Carson said after speaking to someone on the phone. "The techs are done. Now it's just insurance people and security reviewing some new systems."

"Can we go inside?" Anne asked as they passed along the side of the building. The snow had been removed, but the three basement windows glistened with patches of ice.

They rounded the corner to the back alley. Carson said, "No. Everyone needs to stay outside. I'll go in and see what I can find out."

As soon as Carson began

talking with the people inside, Anne stuck her head in the door. The back area was a kitchenette probably used as their breakroom. A door in the corner stood open and it looked like the staircase down into the basement. "Hope, you up for an adventure?"

"Oh, no you don't. The last thing I need is to get arrested for breaking and entering."

"But we're not breaking anything, and the door's open so …" Before waiting for Hope to respond, she slipped into the room and headed down the stairs.

"Oh, geez." She turned to Kandi. "What should I do?"

"Don't worry. Try not to make too much noise. I'm not sure how long we can keep this up though." Kandi launched into a loud Christmas carol and Stewart joined in as Hope waited for her opportunity.

Hope made her way down the stairs into the basement where Anne was behind a stack of boxes. "What are we looking for?"

"Beats me. I just figured that maybe we could get an idea of where to go or what to do from here." She pushed back a set of other boxes and opened the top one. Inside was a bunch of papers. Anne thumbed through them. "Must be old customer receipts." She turned around and sighed. "I don't think we're going to find anything here." She glanced around the room, but something niggled at the back of her mind. "Hope, does anything seem out of place to you?"

"Like what?" Hope looked around.

"I don't know. I just feel like I'm missing something." Anne went over and sat down on a swivel chair next to an area that housed what looked like jewelry repair tools. "Let's try something. I'll close my eyes and you tell me what you see."

"I don't know how—"

"Let's try it." Anne faced the back wall and pointed.

"A stack of boxes. A map of

Colorado. Some file cabinets. The area up to the stairs."

Anne sighed. "Ugh. Nothing." She swiveled in her chair, closed her eyes, and pointed at the far wall.

"Not much on that wall. You've got a broom, mop, and bucket. Cabinet. Windows on either side. That's about it."

Anne popped up from her chair. "That's it!"

"What is?"

"When we were walking up the

path I was looking down in case of slick spots." She held up her fingers. "There are three windows."

Hope looked at the wall. "No. There's only two."

"Let's think about it. It's a jewelry shop. They have to store their inventory at night. Why not do it in a hidden space?" Anne rushed over to the wall and began looking at it. "It would need to be something easy as they'd be using it a lot."

"What about that bookcase?"

Hope and Anne went over to it, but the bookcase was sturdy and full of books. "I don't see any latch and I think you'd see a mark on the floor. She turned to move away and as she did, hit the stack of boxes behind her.

"Did you hear that, Hope?"

"Hear what?"

"Listen." Anne hit the box again.

"Sorry, I don't get—" Anne rushed over and knocked one of the boxes they'd looked into. The sound was very different. "Wait, these are empty." Hope tried to take off a top of the box, but it wouldn't budge. "I think it's glued."

"Wait a minute." Anne rushed around to the other side of the stack of boxes and looked down. "YES!"

"What is it?"

"Stand back!" She pulled and a door revealed an interior room. Shelving held boxes that would protect the jewelry. Anne stepped into the room when she heard a noise.

"Hope, come here. It's Maggie."

In the far corner, Maggie was lying on a pile of blankets. "Maggie, Maggie, can you hear me?." Hope bent down and took Maggie's wrist to check her pulse. After doing that she looked in her eyes. "Drugged. I'm not sure with what, but we need to get an ambulance here right away."

Anne ran from the room and up the stairs. "Kandi, call an ambulance." She rushed into the main showroom. "Carson, we found Maggie. She's been drugged."

"Wait—how?" He responded.

"Later. Come on." She grabbed his hand, and they were followed by the others down the stairs. Hope had managed to get Maggie to a sitting position, but it was evident that she wouldn't be able to speak.

"How did you find this?"

"There were only two windows."

"Okay, I have no idea what that

means, but for now let's focus on Maggie." He knelt down next to Hope. "Do you think she'll be okay?"

"I don't know. She's pretty drugged. It's probably good we found her when we did."

Anne paced back and forth as sirens grew louder. After they loaded Maggie up on the gurney, Anne, Hope, and Carson joined Kandi and Stewart in the back.

Hope spoke, "I think we can rule Maggie out now, but we'll need to wait and talk to her first."

"You need to let the department handle it."

Anne responded, "Fine, but do you want to go get the stolen jewels first?"

Chapter Fifteen

"Do you know where they are?" Carson crossed his arms.

Anne nodded, "I'm pretty sure I do but we need to move fast."

"Why?"

"Because if I'm right, we only have a limited time to get the jewels back." She hurried to the truck. Stewart and the others jumped in the cab and waited for instructions.

"We need to go back to the

main square." Stewart threw the truck in reverse and the truck skidded a bit before he moved it back into drive. Snow had begun falling again and the roads were getting icy.

"Hurry." Anne yelled.

"Okay, I have to go the speed limit. I am hauling a sheriff in this vehicle."

"Stop!" Stewart slammed on the brakes and Anne, along with Carson piled out of the vehicle. "Carson, call Deputy Ruiz. Have him and his men keep tabs on the alley behind those shops facing the square. Especially any exits from the upper stories.”

Carson pulled out his phone and spoke to Ruiz. “Okay, so what now, Sherlock?”

“To the jewels.” The crowds had dispersed around the tree and Anne pointed toward it. “There they are.”

“Where?” He looked at the tree.

“Watch.” She found a rock and threw it toward an ornament. It missed the tree by many feet.

"That's destruction of public property. What are you doing?"

"What if I promise to pay for it if I'm wrong?"

Carson sighed. "We're going to have an exciting life together. How about you tell me which one you want to hit?"

"That one." Anne pointed and handed Carson a rock. He tilted back like he was going to fire off a hard ball before letting the rock find its target. Whack. The ornament broke and as it fell, a large velvet bag dropped into the tree's branches. Anne rushed over and held it up to Carson. "See." She opened the bag which contained a large amount of jewels. "Here you go. And I promise that our lives together will always be exciting."

She handed the bag to Carson before kissing him. "Thanks for trusting me and going along with it."

"Thanks for saying yes. I thought you might string me along for a bit." He chuckled. His phone rang. "Carson."

He listened and then hung up. "They caught Jayson. He was hiding out in the attic of that storefront."

Kandi and Stewart joined them. "We just heard on the radio. You did it. You, like, solved the case that wasn't a case, but it became a case."

"I'm thinking the inspectors may want to see this so if Stewart can take me back to the shop, you can come with us." Carson motioned to Stewart, who nodded.

Anne spoke, "Kandi, you want

to walk home?"

"Sure."

After the guys left, the two women linked arms with each other. The night was crisp, and the snow made for an otherworldly silence as they walked.

"Kandi."

"Yes?" She turned toward Anne.

"Thank you. It was really a very cool gift that you all gave me, and I know it took a lot of effort. I also want to say that I'm sorry for being cranky and—"

"It's okay. I'm so happy that it made you happy. I'm also just really glad we found Maggie." She shivered. "Now, let's pick up the pace cause I'm freezing!"

Chapter Sixteen

Anne had invited everyone over for dinner in celebration of her and Carson's engagement. She'd also asked Maggie, who was still recovering from her traumatic experience. She'd prepared a simple meal of a large salad, fettucine with a cream and caper sauce, and poached salmon. Conversation quickly settled back into the past few weeks' events.

Carson spoke, "I have to say

that even though I'm not crazy about Anne trying to solve mysteries, I appreciate all of your help in keeping her focus on that. Ultimately giving me time to come up with the time and place to propose."

"I have to thank Eliza too. She was the one that said Anne would figure out that jewelry robberies plus theater meant it was all for show."

Anne laughed, "I didn't get that from it, even though I should have. I knew for sure Maggie didn't do it as soon as we went to the store."

"How?" Stewart set down his fork.

"I know." Carson winked at Anne.

"It was the broken glass in the front of the store. First, why would a robber want to call attention to themselves by breaking in from the front? Plus, Maggie didn't need to break in. She could have easily gone in, taken the jewels, and left."

"True, but then the finger would have pointed at her as being the one who'd done it." Hope entered the conversation.

"Possibly. But that showed again that she wouldn't have done it for that exact reason." She spoke to Maggie, "Having met you I knew you were smarter than that. You would have stolen it if you were the thief, but then stayed on. Your disappearance made me start looking at Jayson."

Maggie responded, "Was there something that made you start

thinking that way?"

"What you told me."

"Me? Maggie pointed toward herself. "What did I do?"

"It wasn't what you did. It's what you said. You told me that Jayson was worried financially. That's motive. Of course, he had access to all the jewelry and the knowledge of how to make it look like a burglary so means, as well. But it was you all—" Anne motioned to Kandi and the others, "that gave him the perfect opportunity."

"I agree with you there." Maggie nodded. "Jayson had heard me speaking to Kandi about the mystery and a bit of scavenger hunt to get you into the store to try on engagement rings. I was to invite you in, and we'd go through them while they had someone I'd mark as being suspicious. But then I guess the timing got thrown off or something."

"That's when Kandi and Hope stopped me doing any more snooping by making it where I needed to watch over the Inn."

"Sorry, but that's probably my fault." Carson interjected. "I'd planned to come back sooner and ended up needing to have work done on my vehicle before I could pull the trailer here."

"I am simply delighted that everything turned out well for all concerned." Eliza spoke to the group.

"Yes. Especially you, Maggie. Like, that could have—" Kandi stopped when Anne made a face.

"You're right, Kandi. As you know I'd been going to speak with shop owners and when Jayson heard that, he asked to tag along. He wondered if any of the stores had upper stories or attics that overlooked the town square. He said it'd help him to see the tree from a different angle so that he could tell the crew how to decorate it."

Maggie took in a deep breath before continuing. "He told me that he wanted to get my opinion on some decorations for the shop. We went down to the basement, and he had some things there for us to look at for the event. He'd brought some chai for us and the next thing I remembered was waking up in the hospital."

"I have you to thank for my life." She set a box in front of Anne. "This is for you."

Anne cracked open the box. Inside was the gold bracelet inset with diamonds that she'd admired the first time she'd met Maggie.

She reached out and touched it. "This is lovely, but I can't accept this. It's too much."

"You recovered the stolen jewelry and the insurance company along with the head office saved hundreds of thousands of dollars. They gave the new manager discretion to provide a finder's reward."

"Wow." Anne slipped the bracelet on her wrist and Maggie helped her with the clasp. "I need to send the manager a big thank you."

"No need. You're looking at her." Maggie blushed.

"Oh, congratulations!"

Everyone around the table responded in kind.

"One question." Maggie closed the box. "How did you know where to look for the stolen jewelry?"

"Ah, you can thank Mouser for that. He'd knocked ornaments off my tree and when we set to putting things back, we found something inside one of them. I realized that Jayson would need to hide the jewelry somewhere safe. Where better than where lots of people are milling around? He could keep an eye on it from the upper story. Then he could get it later when the tree came down. I think that was most likely his original plan, but he must have overheard Maggie saying she thought she knew more about the thief. That was her playing her part with me, but he didn't know that.

Of course, the ones at first had been made up, but he had done the real ones later so the jewelry shop would be just another one on the list. He drugged Maggie and then went up to the building to wait until it got late. Then he'd go and take the jewelry in the middle of the night. Chances are no one would be around, but if anyone did come along, he could claim the one for the shop had been damaged and he was repairing it."

"Well, he's sitting in jail now, so he'll have a lot of time to think about what he's done. Robbery, kidnapping, and attempted murder."

Maggie shivered. "I hope he would have told someone I was

there. But I guess we'll never know."

Eliza admired the bracelet on Anne's wrist. "Before I forget, may I ask about the scarf?"

"Was that yours?" Anne leaned back and laughed.

"It's actually a gift for you Anne. We wanted to give you something to serve as a nice memory and as an engagement gift."

"Hold on." Anne went and retrieved the scarf while Kandi brought in flan for dessert and

Hope poured Prosecco in their glasses. They pointed her to the tag. Inside in tiny print it said, "You're always a star to us." Initials surrounded it. Anne felt the tears in her eyes. "All of you are so important to me. Thank you."

"How about a toast?" Carson rose from his seat. He held up the flute. "To Anne. My love. To the mysteries that await us in the years ahead. And to great friends and family."

Everyone agreed and toasted

with each other.

"To presence." Anne lifted her glass.

From the Author

I hope you enjoyed this short Christmas story that introduces you to the residents of Carolan Springs, Colorado. In the story, Anne shares a memory that involved the cartoon character of Mr. Magoo. This is a true story about my mother and father. Every year, we'd search on and around the tree to try and find Mr. Magoo's present to my mother.

My father died just after his 45th birthday and I wish I would have thought to put his last note to my mother inside an ornament for her to have that memory renewed every Christmas. Alas, both are now gone, but the importance of the simple things mean so much later in life. Especially as we have dealt with an exceptionally challenging year (2020) when this book was *published.*

Presents are wonderful, but the presence of loved ones, of cherished friendships that deepen every year, and of new relationships yet to flourish are the greatest gifts. Treasure them.

Merry Christmas and may God bless you and yours.

Vikki

Books by Vikki Walton

A Backyard Farming Series

- Chicken Culprit

- Cordial Killing

- Honey Homicide

- Christmas Capers

- Potager Plot

- Duck Disaster (2022 release)

A Taylor Texas Mystery

- Death Takes A Break

- Death Makes A Move

- Death Stakes A Claim

- Death Steals A Kiss (2022

release)

Viviane's Adventures (Global pet/housesitting mysteries)

- Hijinks in Ajijic
- Deception in Devon